Feodor
Rojankovsky's

Great Big

GOLDEN PRESS • NEW YORK
Western Publishing Company, Inc., Racine, Wisconsin

Animal
Book

1982 Edition

Come see the animals on the farm.

There is a rooster in the chicken coop,

and a hen with her chicks.

There is a cow in the meadow

with her calf.

There is a big pig with two pink piglets,

and there are some geese with two goslings.

The rabbit in the hutch

has four hungry bunnies.

The mother sheep has two lambs.

The mother goat has a kid.

One of the guinea hens has a new chick.

They live in the pen with the turkey.

The mother donkey and her baby

spend all day in the field.

The ducks and the ducklings

swim in the pond.

The mother cat sleeps in the barn with her kittens.

Sometimes the dog wakes them up.

Out in the pasture,

the mother horse grazes with her colt.

Now you have seen all the animals. Come back soon.